There may be some argument about which European first bumped into America—an Italian or a Viking. But of this there is no doubt. The whole world has discovered that jolly Viking, Hagar the Horrible. His misadventures and daring-don't level readers of more than 675 newspapers the world over with laughter every day.

The whole hairy hoard is here: Hagar, the not-so-hard-working barbarian; Helga, the hand that cradles the rock, er, rocks the cradle; Honi, whose heart is yet to be had; Hamlet, the misbegotten heir; and Lucky Eddie, Hagar's sidekick.

Here's your chance to join the more than 35 million people who yuk it up with Hagar, winner of a RUBEN, the National Cartoonists Society's highest tribute.

Hagar the Horrible books from Tempo

HÄGAR
THE HORRIBLE

HELGA'S REVENGE

by Dik Browne

TEMPO BOOKS, NEW YORK

HAGAR THE HORRIBLE: HELGA'S REVENGE

A Tempo Book / published by arrangement with
King Features Syndicate, Inc.

PRINTING HISTORY
Tempo Original / November 1983

ISBN: 0-441-31453-8

Tempo Books are published by The Berkley Publishing Group,
200 Madison Avenue, New York, New York 10016.
Tempo Books are registered in the United States Patent Office.
PRINTED IN THE UNITED STATES OF AMERICA

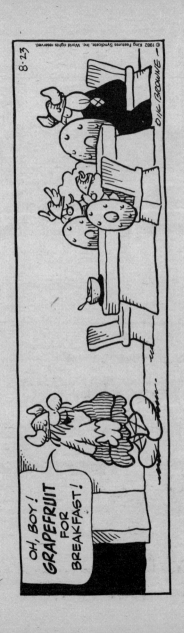

10-13

DIK BROWNE

DIK BROWNE·

11·20

DIK BROWNE 12-20

DIK BROWNE 1-20